# Hookman

## Lauren Yee

A Samuel French Acting Edition

# SAMUEL FRENCH

FOUNDED 1830

SAMUELFRENCH.COM
SAMUELFRENCH-LONDON.CO.UK

## FOR PRODUCTION ENQUIRIES

### UNITED STATES AND CANADA
Info@SamuelFrench.com
1-866-598-8449

### UNITED KINGDOM AND EUROPE
Plays@SamuelFrench-London.co.uk
020-7255-4302

Each title is subject to availability from Samuel French, depending upon country of performance. Please be aware that *HOOKMAN* may not be licensed by Samuel French in your territory. Professional and amateur producers should contact the nearest Samuel French office or licensing partner to verify availability.

## MUSIC USE NOTE

*HOOKMAN* received its world premiere at Encore Theatre Company (Lisa Steindler and James Faerron, co-artistic directors) in association with Z Space Theatre in San Francisco, California on May 9, 2015. The performance was directed by Becca Wolff, with sets by James Faerron, costumes by Christina Dinkel, lights by Joshua McDermott, sound by Drew Yerys, and props and blood effects by Devon LaBelle. The Stage Manager was Kevin Johnson, the Assistant Stage Manager was Amber Bryant. The cast was as follows:

| | |
|---|---|
| **LEXI** | Taylor Jones |
| **JESS** | Sarah Matthes |
| **YOONJI** | Katharine Chin |
| **CHLOE** | Aily Roper |
| **KAYLEIGH** | Jessica Lynn Carroll |
| **HOOKMAN** | Devin O'Brien |

*HOOKMAN* was first presented at Company One Boston Center for the Arts as part of the Double X Festival (Shawn LaCount, Artistic Director) in Boston, Massachusetts on March 23, 2012. The performance was directed by Greg Maraio, with sets by Mike Best, costumes by Cara Pacifico, sound by Edward J. Young, lights by Saulius Szelas, makeup and special effects by Lynn Wilcott, and dramaturgy by Ilana Brownstein. The Production Manager was Karthik Subramanian and the Stage Manager was Marjorie Scarff. The cast was as follows:

| | |
|---|---|
| **LEXI** | Erin Butcher |
| **JESS** | Nicole Prefontaine |
| **YOONJI** | Pearl Shin |
| **CHLOE** | Hannah Cranton |
| **KAYLEIGH** | Mimi Augustin |
| **HOOKMAN** | Joe Kidawski |

*HOOKMAN* was also presented at the University of California San Diego's Baldwin New Play Festival (Naomi Iizuka, head of playwriting) in La Jolla, California on April 19, 2012. The performance was directed by Larissa Lury, with sets by Natalie Khuen, costumes by Mary Rochon, sound by Melanie Chen, and lights by Sy Simms. The Stage Managers were Kristina Beerman and Lindy Luong. The cast was as follows:

LEXI . . . . . . . . . . . . . . . . . . . . . . . . . . . . . . . . . . . . . . . . . . . Sarah Halford

JESS . . . . . . . . . . . . . . . . . . . . . . . . . . . . . . . . . . . . . . . . . . . . Vi Flaten

YOONJI. . . . . . . . . . . . . . . . . . . . . . . . . . . . . . . . . . . . . . . . Mimi Ngo

CHLOE . . . . . . . . . . . . . . . . . . . . . . . . . . . . . . . . . . . . . . .Ngozi Anwanyu

KAYLEIGH. . . . . . . . . . . . . . . . . . . . . . . . . . . . . . . . . . . . .Annalice Heinz

HOOKMAN . . . . . . . . . . . . . . . . . . . . . . . . . . . . . . . . . . . .Matt MacNelly

*HOOKMAN* was commissioned by Encore Theatre Company with support from the Gerbode Foundation.

*HOOKMAN* was also developed at Rattlestick Playwrights Theatre and the Magic Theatre.

# CHARACTERS

**LEXI** – 17, female. Freshman at UConn. An only child.

**JESS** – 18, female. Freshman at UC Davis. Possibly Lexi's best friend. Maternal.

**YOONJI** – 18, female. Freshman at UConn. Lexi's roommate. Korean American. Passive aggressive.

**CHLOE** – 18, female. Freshman at UConn. Carries a large thermos of coffee. Thrilled to be alive.

**KAYLEIGH** – 15, female. Sophomore at West Porter High. On a quiet power trip.

**HOOKMAN** – Old enough to be sketchy, male. Has a hook for a hand. Constantly looks hung over. The actor playing **HOOKMAN** also plays:

> **SEAN** – 20, male. Junior at DePaul University. Plays intramural baseball. May be a rapist.
>
> **ADAM** – 21, male. Senior at UConn. Lexi's residential advisor. The local pot dealer.

# TIME / PLACE

1. In the car / the Friday of Thanksgiving break
2. University of Connecticut
3. West Porter High

# AUTHOR'S NOTE

Avoid the impulse to play Lexi and the other female characters as vapid valley girls. Everyone is very focused and engaged in what they are saying, even if it sounds meaningless. Dialogue should overlap, correct itself, trail off, just randomly end mid-breath.

("Words in parentheses and quotes") denote an emotion and are not dialogue

(Words in parentheses) are dialogue

[Words in brackets] are implied but not spoken out loud

# SPECIAL THANKS

Naomi Iizuka, Adele Edling Shank, Allan Havis, Antje Oegel, and Bailey Williams.

*For Gus*

## Scene

*(In the car.)*

*(A metal scraping sound. Then lights up on JESS and LEXI leaving the In 'N Out drivethru. LEXI drives. JESS in the passenger seat with the tray of fries and her cheeseburger. JESS occasionally feeds fries to LEXI. The Friday after Thanksgiving. An unusually cold Northern California night.)*

**JESS.** So you want to know something weird?

**LEXI.** Did I ask for ketchup?

**JESS.** Yeah, it's

It's right there

**LEXI.** Oh, okay

> *(LEXI has the car at the edge of the parking lot, waits to turn into the street into the oncoming traffic.)*

Which way?

**JESS.** What?

**LEXI.** Which way should I go?

**JESS.** I think you can go either way.

> *(A car pulls up behind LEXI in the parking lot. LEXI freaks out a little.)*

**LEXI.** Jess, can I go?

**JESS.** I don't, um

**LEXI.** Aaaah, I'm just gonna go.

> *(LEXI goes. JESS winces. LEXI gestures to the car behind her that she just cut off.)*

Sorry. Sorry!

(**JESS** *exhales.*)

**LEXI.** It's 11:59.

**JESS.** I know.

(**LEXI** *makes a little upset noise.*)

You wanted to get the In 'N Out!

**LEXI.** I didn't *ask* for the

*You* said we had time.

**JESS.** It's a midnight screening, it's not even midnight yet.

(**LEXI** *makes another, different upset noise.*)

So you want to know something weird?

**LEXI.** What.

**JESS.** So you remember

(*A cell phone rings.*)

**LEXI.** Is that your phone?

**JESS.** Is that my phone?

Yeah, that's my phone.

(**JESS** *goes in search of her phone.*)

**LEXI.** Is it your mom?

**JESS.** No, it's *your* mom.

**LEXI.** Oh weird,

Lemme talk to her.

(**LEXI** *grabs the phone from* **JESS**.*)

Hey, Mom.

Yeah, this is Jess's phone.

Well, you called Jess's phone.

**JESS.** Hi, Mrs. Gellner!

**LEXI.** Jess says hi.

(*to* **JESS**) She says hi back.

**JESS.** I want to come visit you!

Lemme talk to her.

**LEXI.** (*to* **JESS**) She says she's busy.

(*to phone*) Well, you are.

What do you mean "with what?"
We have to go
We have to go!
I'm driving!

**JESS.** Lex, lemme talk to her.

(**LEXI** *hangs up the phone.*)

**LEXI.** She had to go.

**JESS.** I love your mom.

**LEXI.** My mom's crazy. You have no idea.

**JESS.** She sent me a text, the other day.
She was like

**LEXI.** She keeps sending me all these crazy emails
About how kidnappers kidnap you by playing tapes of
babies so you'll be like, "oh, a baby" and

**JESS.** Oh I read about that

**LEXI.** Or like
How they go to parking lots with scissors and hide
under cars
And she's like,
"Watch out for Hookman"

**JESS.** Hookman... ?

**LEXI.** "Don't go with Hookman"

**JESS.** What's Hookman?

**LEXI.** You know
...
"Hookman."

(**JESS** *shrugs: "no idea."*)

Wait, you've
EVERYONE's heard of
– or maybe your mom's not crazy –
But anyway, so
HOOKMAN:
You're driving along

**LEXI.** *(cont.)* Late at night
By yourself and you're a girl
  – I think it's a girl...
Yeah, it's a girl –
And you don't have a boyfriend
And not even a guy friend who likes you but you don't like him enough so you're just friends who helps you move your furniture?
And you're in your car
And someone highbeams you.

> *(Someone highbeams LEXI.)*

Yeah, like that.
But KEEPS highbeaming you and KEEPS following you
And you get really freaked out and you start driving home –

**JESS.** Why're you driving home if that's just gonna let him know where you live now?

**LEXI.** Well, like
No
Let me finish.
So you get home and you run in and you're like,
"Omigod, there's a guy in a car who's gonna kill me,"
But actually all this time, there was ANOTHER GUY in the *backseat* of your car

**JESS.** Ohhh, I've heard this before

**LEXI.** With a HOOK!
For a HAND!
  – Hookman –
Who was trying to kill you
But like
Every time he – Hookman – went up to kill you,
The guy in the car flashed his highbeams
Which, I guess, scared Hookman?
  – which makes no sense, I know, but –

Ultimately, the highbeam guy kills the guy with the hook

Or,

Calls the police or something,

I'm pretty sure,

I don't know.

**JESS**. So what's the point?

**LEXI**. What.

**JESS**. Of the story.

**LEXI**. Exactly! My mom: SO CRAZY.

And I'm like,

First, Hookman's not real, he's just something that happened to people after Vietnam,

And (b.) why're you scaring me if there's nothing I can do about it?

AND sometimes, she'll call me and she'll be like,

"Stay safe,"

And I'm like,

"What makes you think I'm not safe?

And how can I stay safe if I don't even know if I'm safe in the first place?

Like that makes no sense whatsoever basically."

**JESS**. Maybe she's just wondering how you're doing,

That's all.

…

So you want to know something weird?

**LEXI**. Did we get both fries?

**JESS**. I hate how you don't listen to me.

(**LEXI** *hears this.*)

**LEXI**. What?!

**JESS**. That's your problem:

You never listen to people.

Somebody says something and you have no idea what they just said.

**LEXI.** What're you talking about?

**JESS.** One day, I'm going to do that to you.

**LEXI.** What?

**JESS.** I'm just not gonna listen and then you'll know how it feels.

**LEXI.** No! Jess.

What was it?

**JESS.** See? Now I don't even remember!

**LEXI.** Jessss!

I hear what're you saying, I just didn't hear what you said.

Say it again.

**JESS.** It was two things.

**LEXI.** Was it something important?

Was it something about me?

**JESS.** It was about otters?

**LEXI.** Otters?

**JESS.** One was something about otters, I can't remember.

The other thing was –

Oh! So you remember Jiehae?

**LEXI.** …

Oh yeah

She was such a bitch

I used to hate her.

She slapped me once.

**JESS.** She slapped you?

**LEXI.** Not on the face, but yeah.

I mean, she was good at math

But she was such a bitch.

**JESS.** So

Jiehae

You know she died.

*(beat)*

**LEXI**. Omigod, are you serious?

**JESS**. In Peru.

She was taking a year off.

I saw it on Facebook

Right before you picked me up.

**LEXI**. That is so weird!

**JESS**. Are you smiling?

Omigod, Lexi: you're smiling.

**LEXI**. I'm not

I'm not smiling! I'm just –

Peru?!

**JESS**. I know!

**LEXI**. Like BECAUSE it was Peru

Or "Just

Happened to be Peru?"

**JESS**. I don't know!

Nobody does!

**LEXI**. What do you mean "nobody?"

**JESS**. Nobody knows!

Nobody was there!

**LEXI**. But how did it happen?

**JESS**. It didn't say.

> (**LEXI** *seems crushed by this.*)

**LEXI**. What?!

**JESS**. Maybe she just died

In general.

**LEXI**. But how're they supposed to figure out who did it then?

**JESS**. Why does it have to be someone who did it?

**LEXI**. If she died, then SOMEBODY must've

People our age don't just DIE for no reason

– unless you're like Lindsay Lohan or –

People who kill people should be punished.

**LEXI.** *(cont.)*People who kill people should not be allowed to LIVE with their lives.

Someone should be doing something.

**JESS.** Who?

**LEXI.** I don't know who, but SOMEONE.

**JESS.** You didn't even really know her.

You were the one smiling, just now!

**LEXI.** Did she have a boyfriend?

**JESS.** What?

**LEXI.** If she'd had a boyfriend,

This would not have happened.

**JESS.** How do you know she didn't have a boyfriend?

**LEXI.** Girls without boyfriends are targets.

**JESS.** What?!

**LEXI.** At least that's what my dad says.

**JESS.** Omigod, Lex:

Do you always listen to your dad?

**LEXI.** Is that a question?

Yeah. Of course.

If I can't listen to my dad, who else is there?

… well, what do you think it was?

**JESS.** Oh come on, Lex,

Boys hurt other people and girls hurt themselves.

That's just how it is.

>             (**LEXI** *makes a sound of "aw, I don't like that."*)

Her profile's still up.

I'm going to wait till after Christmas to defriend her.

>             (**LEXI** *makes an offended noise/face.*)

*Otherwise* people're going to see that we were friends when we weren't and

– I don't know –

I only friended her because she friended me first, basically.

**LEXI.** You know who really looks like Jiehae? My roommate.

**JESS.** But isn't your roommate

**LEXI.** No, she's Korean

And she looks exactly like her.

From New Jersey!

**JESS.** Oh, I've never met anyone from New Jersey.

**LEXI.** They pump your gas there. FOR YOU.

**JESS.** Really?

**LEXI.** You don't even have to touch it! I might go over and visit her there over spring break.

**JESS.** Wait,

You're not coming back?

**LEXI.** I don't know

… you should come!

**JESS.** Maybe.

…

So you like it there?

**LEXI.** Great. It's great!

**JESS.** Great.

**LEXI.** They've got all these buildings and when I get back, it's supposed to snow!

**JESS.** East coast.

**LEXI.** And they've got pizza and you have to hold it like this –

(**LEXI** *gestures folding a slice of pizza in half.*)

**JESS.** You seem to really like it.

**LEXI.** I do!

I guess I do.

**JESS.** More than here?

You don't wish you'd stayed here?

**LEXI.** What? And go to Davis?

**JESS.** What's wrong with Davis?

**LEXI.** No, Davis is fine, Davis is just… I mean, YOU go to Davis.

**JESS.** I know.

**LEXI.** Not that there's anything wrong with that, it's just –
I like UConn, that's all. They've got snow!

**JESS.** *(re: In 'N Out.)* Though they have don't this.

**LEXI.** True. It's all pizza there.

**JESS.** You want the rest of my milkshake?

**LEXI.** You don't want it?!

**JESS.** Here:
Have mine.
I didn't do anything to it.
(I had a cold, but I think I'm over it… )

> (**LEXI** *tastes* **JESS**'s *milkshake. Eh.*)

You can have the rest.
I know you want it.

**LEXI.** Yeahhhh.
Wait:
How'm I gonna bring two milkshakes into the theater?

**JESS.** Put it in your purse

**LEXI.** What if it spills?

**JESS.** They're not gonna check
They don't care

**LEXI.** Maybe if I hold it?

> (**LEXI** *tries this, and then attempts consolidating the two milkshakes into one cup.*)

**JESS.** Here, let me do it.

**LEXI.** No, no, no, I can –

**JESS.** Lex, just let me do it.

> (**JESS** *takes the two milkshakes from* **LEXI**. *A metal scraping noise. Only* **LEXI** *hears this.*)

**LEXI.** What was that?

**JESS.** What

**LEXI.** That noise.

**JESS.** I didn't hear anything.

**LEXI**. Like

A scraping?

**JESS**. No?

**LEXI**. Oh.

> (**LEXI** *hits something. The car gets jostled.* **JESS** *drops one of the milkshakes on the passenger seat mat.*)

**JESS**. Aaaah!

**LEXI**. Sorry. Sorry!

> (**JESS** *leans over to pick up the milkshake.*)

So you want to know something weird?

> (**JESS** *sits back up, trying to salvage the milkshake remains. She sees something.*)

**JESS**. Lex, watch out!

## Scene

> (**LEXI** *and* **YOONJI**'s *dorm room.*)
>
> (**YOONJI** *sits at her desk, listening to her music. An opened peach Snapple, fresh out of her mini-fridge, is on her desk. She eats from a bag of puffy Korean snacks. There is a care package full of more Korean snacks on her bed.* **LEXI** *enters with her rolling suitcase and the remains of a pie, covered in foil.*)

**LEXI.** Hey

> (**YOONJI** *wordlessly acknowledges* **LEXI**'s *presence.* **LEXI** *unpacks, puts her pie down.*)

I brought a pie!

> (**YOONJI**, *not hearing anything* **LEXI** *has said, sees* **LEXI** *moving.* **YOONJI** *takes off her headphones.*)

**YOONJI.** Did you say something?

**LEXI.** Oh. No. It's just
I brought a pie
You can have some
If you want.

**YOONJI.** You *bought* a pie?

**LEXI.** I *brought* a pie?
From home?
My mom and me, we made it?

**YOONJI.** You took it on the plane?

**LEXI.** Yeah.

**YOONJI.** Like that?

> (**LEXI** *becomes self-conscious of her pie.*)

**LEXI.** Yes… ?

**YOONJI.** Is it still good?

**LEXI.** I think it's still good.
Yeah, it's still good.
You want some?

**YOONJI.** *(shrugs)* Sure.

**LEXI.** Let me just find something to cut it with.

**YOONJI.** I think I've got something. Over by the – *(gestures)* somewhere.

> *(**YOONJI** puts her headphones back on. **LEXI** searches briefly, then stops.)*

**LEXI.** – so, um, my friend died.

> *(**YOONJI** thinks she's heard something. She's not sure.)*

Over break.

> *(**YOONJI** takes off her headphones.)*

**YOONJI.** Did you say something?

**LEXI.** No, just
My friend
Died
The other day
Over break.
Jess.

> *(No response.)*

**YOONJI.** Wait, the one who went to *Davis?*
She *died?!*

**LEXI.** Yeah.

> *(**YOONJI** sees her life passing before her eyes.)*

**YOONJI.** That, sucks.

> *(**YOONJI** gets up. She's still wearing her headphones, they pull her back. She takes them off clumsily and gets up to hug **LEXI**. **LEXI** inadvertently moves the wrong way. **YOONJI** stops before hugging **LEXI**, instead just kind of stands nearby and folds her arms.)*

**YOONJI.** *(cont.)* So
...
Are you okay?

**LEXI**. Yeah,

Though

… can I get a Snapple?

> (**LEXI** *gestures to the half-drunk peach Snapple on* **YOONJI**'s *desk.*)

**YOONJI**. Oh. Yeah. Sure.

> (**YOONJI** *goes into her mini-fridge, hands her a lemon Snapple.* **LEXI** *looks at* **YOONJI**'s *peach Snapple.*)

**LEXI**. Can I get a peach one, though?

**YOONJI**. Oh

Um

Yeah.

> (**YOONJI** *grudgingly trades* **LEXI** *her peach Snapple.*)

**LEXI**. Thanks.

**YOONJI**. I mean:

Your friend died!

> (**LEXI** *drinks the cold peach Snapple. Mmm.*)

How did it happen?

**LEXI**. We were going to the movies and,

This guy?

This drunk driver?

Just blew through a red light and hit us.

**YOONJI**. Omigod.

**LEXI**. He's okay

… though he did lose a hand.

**YOONJI**. Did he get it back?

**LEXI**. I don't know… ?

**YOONJI**. Or did they have to give him a hook for a hand?

**LEXI**. Wait, like

Hookman?!

**YOONJI**. Hookman… ?

**LEXI**. I mean,
Yeah, that's probably what they did.

**YOONJI**. Omigod, that's horrible...
... having a hook for a hand.

> (**YOONJI** *imagines a hook for a hand, is sad.*)

I bet your insurance would have to be really bad for you
to get a hook for a hand.

**LEXI**. Maybe.

**YOONJI**. What's going to happen to him?

**LEXI**. I don't know, they wouldn't tell me, but uh
They have him. In custody.
In the hospital.
They said they'd call if there's anything else.
So. Good.
For now.

**YOONJI**. What was your friend's last name?

**LEXI**. Gelman. Jess Gelman.
But you want to know something weird?

**YOONJI**. *(types)* Hm.

> (*While* **LEXI** *says the following,* **YOONJI** *searches
> around on her laptop, reads an article.*)

**LEXI**. And it's crazy, but
Getting on the plane, I thought I saw
– I mean, he's in a coma now
So obviously not, but –
I thought I saw the drunk guy
ALSO get on the plane?
Which is so weird.

**YOONJI**. For a guy to get on a plane?

**LEXI**. No, like
Um
It's just nice to be home, that's all.

> (**YOONJI** *looks around.*)

**YOONJI.** I thought you lived in California.

**LEXI.** I do.

**YOONJI.** Then how is this home?

**LEXI.** Just like, school home, you know.
      With school friends.

**YOONJI.** Oh.

**LEXI.** So: good to be back!

**YOONJI.** But you'll go back for your friend's thing, right?

**LEXI.** What?

**YOONJI.** *(re: laptop)* The memorial they're having.

**LEXI.** Wait,
      How do you know about that?

         (**YOONJI** *angles her laptop away from* **LEXI***.)*

**YOONJI.** No, no, no, go on.
      Sorry, go on.

**LEXI.** No, that's it.
      Jess's mom keeps calling me, asking me to come back
      to speak at the thing,
      But then I feel like everyone's just gonna ask me all
      these questions
      And
      My mom said I didn't have to, so –
      I'm back.
      Though I DID send her a text,
      Jess's mom.
      …
      Don't tell anyone.
      I don't really want to talk about it.

**YOONJI.** Oh
      Totally.
      (But I can post it, right?)

**LEXI.** Post what?

         (**YOONJI** *clicks on something, shuts her laptop.)*

**YOONJI.** Though it's good that you guys weren't friends.

**LEXI.** What?

**YOONJI.** What?

**LEXI.** Who said that?

**YOONJI.** You.

**LEXI.** No.

… I mean, I may have said we weren't like BEST friends. That's all.

**YOONJI.** Oh.

Okaaay.

So: "it's good that you weren't best friends."

**LEXI.** Right.

You want to grab some dinner?

**YOONJI.** Oh, no, we're going out to dinner.

**LEXI.** … oh.

**YOONJI.** You should come!

**LEXI.** Really?

**YOONJI.** Yeah! Your friend died!

**LEXI.** She did.

**YOONJI.** Allie's boyfriend is giving us a ride.

**LEXI.** In a car?

**YOONJI.** Yes?

**LEXI.** Driving?

**YOONJI.** We're going to Costco and then we're going to Olive Garden for dinner.

**LEXI.** Um, that's okay

I'll just

Run across the quad and grab something in the dining hall.

**YOONJI.** *(shrugs)* Okay.

> (**YOONJI** *looks around, as if to see what is making* **LEXI** *so busy.*)

**LEXI.** I have to talk to Sean anyway.

**YOONJI**. Who?

**LEXI**. The guy.

**YOONJI**. Oh, HIM!

Are you guys still together?

**LEXI**. … I think so?

Yeah!

**YOONJI**. Wait, so what about the other guy?

**LEXI**. What other guy?

**YOONJI**. Your friend.

The one who came by just now?

**LEXI**. I don't know what you're talking about.

**YOONJI**. Is he a grad student?

'Cause he kind of looked like a grad student.

**LEXI**. What guy?

**YOONJI**. The guy with a, uh

– what do you call it? –

> (**YOONJI** *mimes something that might be misconstrued as "hook for a hand."*)

**LEXI**. Hook for a hand?

**YOONJI**. *(beat)* No?

He just… had a hand for a hand, I think.

**LEXI**. Oh.

**YOONJI**. But anyway! He left something for you.

> (**LEXI** *looks around amid the mess on her bed. She finds a note written in bloody red letters stabbed to her pillow with a knife.*)

**LEXI**. Omigod, Yoonji.

**YOONJI**. Hm?

**LEXI**. LOOK.

**YOONJI**. Oh, you found the knife!

**LEXI**. What?

**YOONJI**. For your pie. The one in the – *(gestures vaguely)* somewhere.

*(**LEXI** realizes she's holding the knife over the pie.)*

**LEXI.** Right.

So the guy who came by

**YOONJI.** The grad student?

**LEXI.** What did he say?

**YOONJI.** Oh, I told him I didn't know when you were coming back.

He said it was okay,

He said he'd come back for you.

**LEXI.** He did?

**YOONJI.** He said he'll be waiting.

You can probably still catch him if you want.

I bet he's still outside.

**LEXI.** That's all right.

*(**LEXI** notices that her pie seems to be full of blood. Or maybe cherry filling! She sets it aside/dumps it. **YOONJI** gets a text.)*

**YOONJI.** Ooohh, that's them.

You sure?

**LEXI.** I'm not that hungry anyway.

(I just didn't eat anything all day... )

**YOONJI.** Okaaay.

*(**YOONJI** almost exits.)*

Wait, were you done?

**LEXI.** What.

**YOONJI.** Your friend

She died.

**LEXI.** Oh

Yeah.

That's it, I guess.

**YOONJI.** Cool.

*(**YOONJI** exits. **LEXI**'s phone rings. She jumps. Oh wait, just her phone. Whew. She checks her*

*phone, silences it, hides her phone. She wipes the knife clean, stashes it under her pillow. Beat.* **LEXI** *waits, then grabs handfuls of puffy Korean snacks from* **YOONJI**'s *care package.)*

## Scene

(**LEXI** and **YOONJI**'s dorm room.)

(**LEXI** asleep on her bed, surrounded by Korean snack wrappers. A menacing figure stands above **LEXI**, brandishing something. **LEXI** wakes up.)

**LEXI**. Aaah!

(Maybe **LEXI** fumbles for the knife under her pillow. It's **CHLOE**, who juggles a petition clipboard and a giant thermos of coffee, pen raised in the air.)

**CHLOE**. HEY!

**LEXI**. Heyyyyy.

(If **LEXI** has the knife, she is lowering it because that's super weird.)

**CHLOE**. How's it going?!
    Fancy seeing you. With all your snacks!

**LEXI**. Oh, these aren't mine,
    These are just Korean –

**CHLOE**. What is going on, why haven't I seen you lately?

**LEXI**. Break?

**CHLOE**. Break. I know.
    CrAzy.
    We should get coffee sometime.

**LEXI**. Yeah!

**CHLOE**. Actually, I'm having coffee with Paloma.
    Do you know Paloma?
    You know Paloma.

(**LEXI** doesn't know this Paloma.)

You've probably
SOMEWHERE!

(**CHLOE** laughs. **LEXI** looks around.)

You should meet her.
You'd like her.

**CHLOE.** She does environmental stuff.
  You do that, right?

**LEXI.** No?

**CHLOE.** Well, SOMEBODY told me you do something good.

**LEXI.** I might want to do Habitat for Humanity?

**CHLOE.** That's probably
  I bet that's it.
  You want to sign my petition?

  *(**LEXI** wonders: "for what?")*

**LEXI.** Sure!

**CHLOE.** It's not for bombs, I promise!

**LEXI.** I like bombs!

  *(**CHLOE** laughs. **LEXI** laughs with her. **LEXI** signs the petition.)*

**CHLOE.** Be careful, it leaks.

  *(Oh shoot, the pen is leaking red ink a little bit.)*

**LEXI.** Oh! Yeah, it kind of –

  *(**LEXI** gets distracted and forgets to hand the pen back to **CHLOE**.)*

**CHLOE.** *And* we're having a protest later.

**LEXI.** For what?

**CHLOE.** You should come.
  You should TOTALLY
  TOTALLY come.

**LEXI.** I don't know, I'm not
  I'm *really* busy.

**CHLOE.** Omigod, tell me about it!
  Remind me of your name again?

**LEXI.** Lexi.

**CHLOE.** LEXI.
  I know this!
  *(re: self)* Chloe.

**LEXI.** Chloe!

**CHLOE.** Lexi. LEXI. So HOW WAS BREAK?

**LEXI.** It was good.

Well

My friend died, the other day.

(**CHLOE** *is distracted, maybe by something on her phone.*)

**CHLOE.** What?

**LEXI.** My friend, died?

**CHLOE.** *(still on her phone)* Huh?

**LEXI.** No, it's okay.

**CHLOE.** No, no, no, say it again

**LEXI.** My friend?

She DIED?

*(Beat,* **CHLOE** *computes.)*

**CHLOE.** Ohhhh, your FRIEND died.

I thought you said your PHONE died.

And I was like,

Was I supposed to call her?

Because my phone? WORST PHONE ever.

You have a Samsung? – don't ever get a Samsung.

*(shakes head)* Koreans.

But riiiight, LEXI, I heard about that.

**LEXI.** What?

**CHLOE.** The drunk driver,

The guy who hit you?

**LEXI.** Wait, where did you hear that from?

**CHLOE.** From you.

**LEXI.** From me?

**CHLOE.** You posted about it on your wall, right?

**LEXI.** … no?

**CHLOE.** The article? In the paper?

**LEXI.** What article?

**CHLOE.** Oh well,

> Maybe someone else did then.
>
> But what're you going to do about it?

**LEXI.** About my wall?

**CHLOE.** About your friend.

**LEXI.** Is there something I should be doing about it?

**CHLOE.** You could start a petition.

**LEXI.** *("no")* My printer's running out of ink.

**CHLOE.** Oh no, you can just do it online!

**LEXI.** Maybe then.

**CHLOE.** When my little sister died, I did the exact same thing.

> And it helped. A lot.

**LEXI.** Oh, okay.

**CHLOE.** Or you could write a book.

**LEXI.** I don't really write books.

**CHLOE.** Have you read *The Year of Magical Thinking* by Joan Didion?

**LEXI.** No?

**CHLOE.** I was reading about it the other day,

> On TV.
>
> Michelle Williams was talking about it
>
> Talking about Heath Ledger,
>
> And it was really uplifting,
>
> To hear her talk about reading it.

**LEXI.** Oh, maybe.

**CHLOE.** But I'm sure you'll get what's coming to you.

> The truth has a way of making itself known.

**LEXI.** What?

**CHLOE.** What.

**LEXI.** What did you say?

**CHLOE.** What did I just say, I have no idea what I just said.

> (**CHLOE** *laughs to cover up the awkwardness. She looks for something else to comment on.*)

**CHLOE**. *(cont.)*I have those shoes.

I have those

Exact

Same

Shoes!

(**CHLOE** *realizes she's wearing those shoes.*)

And I'm WEARING THEM RIGHT NOW!

(**CHLOE** *and* **LEXI** *have a moment of "omigod, we are!" togetherness.*)

Anyway! Nice to see you.

**LEXI**. Yeah!

**CHLOE**. We should hang out some time!

(**LEXI** *thinks she hears something.*)

**LEXI**. Wait!

**CHLOE**. What?

**LEXI**. Please don't go!

**CHLOE**. I have a protest.

**LEXI**. We should hang out! Get some coffee!

(**CHLOE** *wrenches the petition out of* **LEXI**'*s grip.*)

**CHLOE**. I have coffee. Tomorrow!

**LEXI**. Tomorrow?

**CHLOE**. (Maaaaybe... )

Email me!

I gotta go. (I am SO late.)

(**CHLOE** *exits.*)

**LEXI**. Wait! You forgot your –

(*The pen explodes red ink all over* **LEXI**.)

– pen.

## Scene

(**LEXI** and **YOONJI**'s dorm room.)

(**LEXI** on Skype with **SEAN**. Throughout this scene, **LEXI** tries to get the red ink stains off her hands, just out of **SEAN**'s view. And also tries to not stain the laptop. **SEAN** multitasks.)

**LEXI.** – right?

**SEAN.** Huh?

No. Say it again.

I wasn't

What did you say?

**LEXI.** I went through the WHOLE ARTICLE and it barely talks about me!

It talks about the accident, the drunk driver, Jess, the memorial, the whole thing but almost nothing about me!

**SEAN.** What accident?

**LEXI.** The one I was in. With Jess.

**SEAN.** And Jess is the friend?

**LEXI.** Yes.

**SEAN.** And what is this?

**LEXI.** The article. The article on my friend.

**SEAN.** Jess.

**LEXI.** YES.

And I'm like, WHY would someone post this on my wall if it's not even about me? Or mentions me?

**SEAN.** I don't, uh…

**LEXI.** And you want to know what's really stupid?

(**SEAN** makes a face/noise: "uhh, no, but you're going to tell me anyway, so yeah.")

It even talks with this other girl – her roommate from college – who wasn't even there!

*(At some point during* **LEXI***'s speaking,* **SEAN** *begins IMing with someone else who IMed him first.)*

**LEXI**. *(cont.)*And *then*

It says

They're having this *roommate girl* say stuff at the memorial!

And I know I said I didn't want to make a speech

Because you know, I'm not a good public speaker.

    **(SEAN** *had no idea this was the case.)*

**SEAN**. Okay.

**LEXI**. But just because I said I wasn't speaking doesn't mean you have to go find some roommate girl she didn't even know

To speak instead!

'Cause Jess and me, we knew each other from seventh grade till freshman year

Which is like,

Eight, nine

    **(LEXI** *actually counts the years in her mind.)*

*Six* straight years we were friends

Out of seventeen years on this planet?

**SEAN**. Seventeen?

**LEXI**. And so, maybe it's just me, but like

One semester

  – not even one semester! –

Of knowing her?

That's like –

**SEAN**. I thought you were eighteen.

**LEXI**. I mean, one day.

But you know?!

**SEAN**. Yeah.

Though

Maybe she changed.

**LEXI.** What?

**SEAN.** What.

**LEXI.** What did you say?

**SEAN.** I don't know, like

> (*An IM ping from* **SEAN**'s *computer. He mutes his computer. Ping. Oh, wait that won't work. He searches for the correct window. Another ping.*)

Maybe

Maybe she had a really good friendship with her other friend, I don't know.

Or maybe, like

She had it [ping] coming.

Like I heard you could see him [ping] coming?

**LEXI.** What?

**SEAN.** Or maybe she'll come around.

Maybe eventually

She'll see the light.

**LEXI.** She's dead.

How can she see the light if she's dead?

> (**SEAN** *makes a face: "I was just trying to make you feel better."*)

**SEAN.** Oh. Okay.

> (*They reach a standstill.*)

**LEXI.** So

How was home?

> (**SEAN** *really wants to look at his IM. He resists.*)

**SEAN.** What?

Oh. Good, it was uh –

> (*For a moment, the screens freeze. Which means* **SEAN** *freezes and* **LEXI** *waits for* **SEAN** *to unfreeze. Little bits of future* **SEAN** *replace old* **SEAN** *on the screen, creating some in-between image of him.*)

– basically. Yeah.

**LEXI.** Sorry. It

**SEAN.** What?

**LEXI.** My internet's been really weird.

**SEAN.** Okay.

**LEXI.** Are you sick?

**SEAN.** Yeah, I got a cold.

**LEXI.** Awww.

Me, too.

**SEAN.** Really?

**LEXI.** Well, not yet

But the flu's going around

So just a matter of time till it gets to me!

(**SEAN** *finishes the end of a burrito.*)

Is that a burrito?

**SEAN.** Yeah.

**LEXI.** Is it good?

**SEAN.** I think so… ?

**LEXI.** I love burritos.

**SEAN.** You should get one.

**LEXI.** I was, but I wanted to make sure I caught you.

**SEAN.** Yeahhhh.

**LEXI.** I missed you, Sean.

(**SEAN** *is uncomfortable.*)

**SEAN.** Yeahh. Like / people I never see people when I'm supposed to –

**LEXI.** Like I was actually almost was gonna call you

(*They realize they are speaking over each other, wait for the other to speak. They make little sputtering noises and say variations on "oh, no, you go."*)

**SEAN.** So

How's your arm?

**LEXI.** Oh, it's fine.

You can't see it now.

It's fading.

**SEAN.** Sorry about that.

**LEXI.** I had a nice time.

**SEAN.** Yeah, huh.

**LEXI.** Though not that I'm sensitive or anything
But I kind of wish you'd've asked first.

**SEAN.** What?

**LEXI.** I probably would've said yes so like
No big deal but
*(swallows)* You kind of forced me.

**SEAN.** Really?
'Cause
I don't think I did.
Yeah
I don't think I did.

**LEXI.** I'm not gonna say anything,
Just
You kind of did.

**SEAN.** I don't remember that.

**LEXI.** But, um
Do you know when you're coming again?

**SEAN.** Yeah, um
I was thinking:
And Chicago's really far from Connecticut and I don't
know how often I'm gonna get out there anymore and,
over break
I think Katie and I got back together
I think, is what happened
… if that's okay.

**LEXI.** Oh. No.
We're not

**SEAN.** You sure?

**LEXI.** Yeah.
Don't worry about it.

**SEAN.** Cool.

**LEXI**. I'm kind of seeing this other guy anyway.

**SEAN**. Oh
   Awesome!

**LEXI**. My RA. From New Hampshire.

   (**SEAN** *has no idea what New Hampshire is like.*)

   It's a swing state.

**SEAN**. Oh, okay.

**LEXI**. He's going to be a lawyer,
   Like my dad.

**SEAN**. I love lawyers!

**LEXI**. And I'm probably going to Egypt for spring break anyway.

**SEAN**. Oh. Have fun.
   I hear there's a lot of, stuff there.
   Lemme know if you ever visit, though.
   We might get a couch soon.

**LEXI**. Cool.

**SEAN**. But have a good year!
   It was cool meeting you.
   Say hi to my brother for me.

**LEXI**. I have class with him, on Mondays.

**SEAN**. Cool. Take care of yourself now.

**LEXI**. Yeah.

**SEAN**. Stay safe!

   (**SEAN** *signs off.* **LEXI** *closes her laptop. A sudden, strange noise.* **LEXI** *jumps. Wait, that's her phone. Oh, it's her phone again. Didn't she just silence this? She looks at her phone.*)

## Scene

*(In the car.)*

*(**JESS** in the passenger seat, **LEXI** in the driver's seat, with In 'N Out as before. Mid-conversation.)*

**JESS.** You want the rest of my milkshake?

**LEXI.** You don't want it?!

**JESS.** Here:

Have mine.

I didn't do anything to it.

(I had a cold, but I think I'm over it.)

*(**LEXI** tastes **JESS**'s milkshake. Eh.)*

You can have the rest.

I know you want it.

**LEXI.** Yeahhhh.

Wait:

How'm I gonna bring two milkshakes into the theater?

**JESS.** Put it in your purse

**LEXI.** What if it spills?

**JESS.** They're not gonna check

They don't care

**LEXI.** Maybe if I hold it?

*(**LEXI** tries this, and then attempts consolidating the two milkshakes into one cup.)*

**JESS.** Here, let me do it.

**LEXI.** No, no, no, I can –

**JESS.** Lex, just let me do it.

*(**JESS** takes the two milkshakes from **LEXI**. **LEXI** hits something. The car gets jostled. **JESS** drops one of the milkshakes on the passenger seat mat.)*

Aaaah!

**LEXI.** Sorry. Sorry!

(JESS *leans over to pick up the milkshake. A metal scraping noise. Only* LEXI *hears this.*)

LEXI. What was that?

JESS. What

LEXI. That noise.

JESS. I didn't hear anything.

LEXI. Like
A scraping?

JESS. No?

LEXI. So you want to know something weird?

(JESS *sits back up, trying to salvage the milkshake remains.*)

JESS. Where're the napkins?

LEXI. They're in the
Somewhere, back there.

JESS. Where?

LEXI. I don't know.

…

Soooo
(*"isn't this awkward/funny?"*) I think I was raped the other day.

(JESS, *still looking for the napkins, can't hear her.*)

JESS. What?

LEXI. I think
(*louder*) I might've been, RAPED?
The other day.

JESS. Wait, WHAT?
That's not okay.
Lexi, that is not okay.
Do you want to talk about this?

LEXI. I don't know.

JESS. We don't have to talk about this if you don't want to talk about this, but we should talk about this,

**JESS**. *(cont.)* You should pull this car over
  – as soon as you –

          (**LEXI** *keeps driving.*)

  Was it someone you know?
  'Cause it's usually someone you know.
  Are you pregnant?

**LEXI**. No!

**JESS**. No?

**LEXI**. He was wearing a condom, jeez.
  I'm not stupid.

**JESS**. Oh.
  That was nice of him.
  Who was it?

**LEXI**. It's no one you know.

**JESS**. Okay, then tell me.
  …
  I will tell your mom.

**LEXI**. Why would you tell my mom?

**JESS**. I will tell your mom if you don't tell me!

**LEXI**. Don't tell my mom!

**JESS**. Then tell me!
  Did this happen at school?

**LEXI**. *(small)* Yes.

**JESS**. Ohhhh, Lex!
  I KNEW this would happen!

**LEXI**. What?

**JESS**. People on the East Coast!

**LEXI**. No, that's not –

**JESS**. This is
  This is what happens when you go outside.

**LEXI**. It wasn't outside –

**JESS**. Were you wearing something?

**LEXI**. Huh?

**JESS**. Was it the
    Thing?
    With the straps?
    What was he like?
    Was he cute or was he gross?
    (Was he gross?)

**LEXI**. Why would he be gross?

**JESS**. I don't know, rapists're gross.

**LEXI**. He wasn't gross.

**JESS**. You're sure?

**LEXI**. I'm sure.

**JESS**. Was he a student?
    Was he

**LEXI**. I don't know
    I don't know!

**JESS**. What do you mean you don't know?!
    Like you don't know *him*?

**LEXI**. I don't know!
    He just did it and I didn't see him at all.

**JESS**. At all.

**LEXI**. No, okay?

**JESS**. Okay, but –
    I thought you said he was cute.

**LEXI**. What?

**JESS**. You just said

**LEXI**. NO.
    And like I don't even know if it was,
    Rape to begin with.

**JESS**. Okay, and –
    I'm going to believe you
    But:
    People don't like it when people're rapists
    But they also REALLY don't like it when people accuse
    people of being rapists.

(**LEXI** *is pointedly silent.*)

**JESS.** *(cont.)*Lex?

**LEXI.** You're kind of making me feel bad about this.

**JESS.** What?!

How'm I –

(**JESS** *looks over, notices that* **LEXI** *is crossing the threshold of crying.*)

Oh shit.

Lex, I'm sorry, did I

Do you need a hug?

Does it make it worse if I hold you or if I don't hold you?

Here:

I'm going to hold you.

(**JESS** *gives* **LEXI** *the most heartfelt, most complete hug she can before the light turns green and* **LEXI** *has to continue driving.*)

Do you need a tissue?

**LEXI.** There's usually some in the glove compartment.

**JESS.** Okay.

(**JESS** *checks, finds a small cocktail napkin. She smushes it up to make it softer, then hands it to* **LEXI,** *rubs* **LEXI** *on the back.* **LEXI** *has a sad moment, then –* )

**LEXI.** Shoot. We missed the entrance.

**JESS.** We did?

**LEXI.** I'll just go around and get on in a couple blocks.

**JESS.** Oh, okay.

See?

You're so good at this.

You just got your license and you are so good at this!

(**LEXI** *has a small, proud moment. She is good at this.*)

**LEXI.** *(small)* Yeah.

**JESS.** See? I knew you could do this.

**LEXI.** I don't know what I was so scared of!

**JESS.** And next time: it's gonna be better.

> (**LEXI** *shrugs.*)

YES:

It's gonna be ten times better.

'Cause you know,

"It gets better."

**LEXI.** Yeah, but only if you're gay.

**JESS.** True.

**LEXI.** He really did come out of nowhere.

**JESS.** I know.

And I'm glad you told me.

**LEXI.** Yeah?

**JESS.** Yeah.

**LEXI.** But can we not talk about this anymore?

**JESS.** Done!

You want me to drive?

**LEXI.** No, that's okay.

**JESS.** You sure?

**LEXI.** Yeah.

> (**LEXI** *notices something on* **JESS**'s *shirt. A small red stain.*)

Oh Jess, you got a –

On your –

**JESS.** Oh shoot.

> (**LEXI** *licks her finger, rubs the blood off with her finger, tastes.*)

Is it?

**LEXI.** … mm?

**JESS.** Ketchup?

**LEXI.** … no.

**JESS.** It's probably just my period.

**LEXI.** Oh,

I thought so.

I could kind of smell it.

**JESS.** Oh, ew.

**LEXI.** What?!

I know how it smells:

It smells nice!

It smells like me!

**JESS.** It's the worst part about being a girl.

**LEXI.** *("no, it isn't")* Pregnancy!

Menopause!

And all the stuff people'll do to you *'cause* you're a girl

**JESS.** Though you don't have to worry about a penis!

**LEXI.** I know!

It'd be so weird if I had a penis.

I wouldn't know what to do with it!

**JESS.** Right?!

**LEXI.** I'd be like –

>        (**LEXI** *makes a "what will I do with this penis*
>        *upon me?!" face/noise.*)

**JESS.** Yeahhh

**LEXI.** Do you think guys worry about things like this?

>        (**JESS** *contemplates.*)

Do you think guys worry about, like:

"Am I pretty enough?

Am I good enough?

Will I ever have worth as a person?"

**JESS.** No.

**LEXI.** Yeah, me neither.

How'd it get on your shirt, though?

**JESS.** I get my period and that stuff gets all over.

LEXI. I know, right?!

Once

I was staying over at these people's houses and I got out of the shower

And like –

JESS. Ew, Lex.

> (**LEXI** *and* **JESS** *are amused by this line of conversation.*)

LEXI. They had this WHITE bath mat rug thing?

WHO gets a white bath mat rug thing?!

JESS. Oh c'mon, I'm eating! I'm eating!

LEXI. They still haven't said anything,

So either they didn't notice or – !

> (**LEXI** *imagines what the possibilities might be.*)

JESS. *(fondly)* Lexi, you are gross

You are SO GROSS.

LEXI. Yeahhh.

So you want to know something weird?

> (*The blood stain on* **JESS** *'s shirt begins to spread as* **JESS** *continues to bleed.* **LEXI** *is too pleased to notice.*)

JESS. What.

LEXI. It's just

I thought you would change.

JESS. You're the one at Yukon.

You're the one who left.

LEXI. No, but like

I was so worried you'd come back and you'd drink or something.

JESS. *(dismissive)* No.

I mean, not a lot.

LEXI. Or that we wouldn't see each other anymore.

**JESS.** We see each other.
>   We see each other a LOT.
>   And still my mom says, "Oh, you should hang out,
>   You should get together."
>   And I'm like,
>   "WE DO."
>   Not like I don't like to
>   But WE DO.
>   I don't mind
>   But it kind of makes it hard to see other people
>   When you want to hang out but you don't want to hang
>   out with other people.

**LEXI.** I just like it better when it's just us
>   It's more fun that way.

**JESS.** Yeah, but sometimes
>   It's just more convenient to hang out in a group, you
>   know?

**LEXI.** I guess,
>   I don't know.

**JESS.** Oh! Also, I won't need a ride back, after.
>   I'm getting brunch.

**LEXI.** With who?

**JESS.** Just some people from school.
>   Some of the Davis people who live around here.

**LEXI.** AFTER the movie?

**JESS.** It's kind of our thing.

**LEXI.** And why would you want to see Davis people during
>   break?

**JESS.** You can come if you want.
>   You won't know anybody, but you can come.

>       (**LEXI** *doesn't respond.*)

>   Okay:
>   Why're you upset?

**LEXI.** I'm not

I'm not upset.

It's just

Then why're we even hanging out?

**JESS.** See, I knew this would happen.

I knew you would –

**LEXI.** What?

**JESS.** You never change.

**LEXI.** Why would I change?

And I go to UConn.

How can I not be the type of person who changes if I go to UConn?

**JESS.** Yeah, right,

"Yukon."

**LEXI.** I might want to go to grad school.

I might want to do Teach for America.

**JESS.** Why?

**LEXI.** To Teach. America.

**JESS.** You?

**LEXI.** … yes?

(Though, why not?)

**JESS.** You're an only child.

**LEXI.** What does that mean?

**JESS.** "You're an only child."

That's all.

**LEXI.** But you said it like –

**JESS.** You only think of yourself and you never think about other people, that's all.

**LEXI.** I do things.

**JESS.** For people?

**LEXI.** … yes?

**JESS.** When?

**LEXI.** I don't know. I don't keep track of it like some sort of person like that.

**JESS.** It's just not in your nature.

You just don't know how to do the right thing.

**LEXI.** Wait, what're we talking about?

**JESS.** Davis?

**LEXI.** What about Davis?

**JESS.** I only went to Davis because you were going to go.

I only went to Davis so we could go together.

**LEXI.** … I don't remember that.

**JESS.** (*"See!"*)

**LEXI.** No.

**JESS.** Lex, it's not your fault,

It's just

Who You Are.

(**JESS** *bleeds more.*)

**LEXI.** Wait, Jess.

That's not your period.

**JESS.** You haven't seen me on my period.

(**LEXI** *looks around the car. The frontage road. In 'N Out. Déjà vu.*)

**LEXI.** We've done this before.

**JESS.** We do this all the time:

We always get In 'N Out and drive to the movies at the mall.

(**LEXI**, *still weirded out, tries to relax.*)

I was gonna say something.

**LEXI.** What.

**JESS.** I don't remember, but it was two things…

**LEXI.** Was it something important?

Was it something about me?

…

Was it about otters?

**JESS.** Otters?

**LEXI.** Was one of the things something about otters?

**JESS**. Yeah, actually. I can't think of it right now, but yeah, it was.

The other thing was –

**LEXI**. Jiehae.

**JESS**. … mm?

**LEXI**. The something weird was something about Jiehae

**JESS**. YES! JIEHAE!

**LEXI**. *(aware of the repeat)* She was such a bitch

I used to hate her.

She slapped me once.

Not on the face, but yeah.

**JESS**. Exactly!

**LEXI**. Let's go home.

**JESS**. I don't know!

Nobody does!

**LEXI**. Which way?

Jess, do you hear me?

**JESS**. Nobody: nobody knows!

Nobody was there!

**LEXI**. Jess!

**JESS**. What?

**LEXI**. Did you hear me?

**JESS**. You don't want to see the movie?

**LEXI**. I want to go home and I don't want to see the movie.

Which way?

**JESS**. I think you can go either way.

> (**LEXI** *pulls into a gas station, and uses it to make a U-turn.* **LEXI** *sighs in relief as she watches their intended path get farther away. Then* **LEXI** *notices they're going way too fast. They fly over a speed bump.*)

**LEXI**. Jess, we're going too fast.

> (**LEXI** *tries to stop the car.*)

**JESS**. I know, right?

> (**LEXI** *looks at the road.*)

**LEXI**. This is the way to the mall.

 This is the way to the movies.

 We're still going to the movies.

**JESS**. Yeah, we're going to the movies.

**LEXI**. Jess, help me.

 Help me.

> (**JESS** *looks out her window.*)

**JESS**. Omigod, look at that.

 Wow.

 I wonder

 I wonder what they did.

 Look at that girl's car.

**LEXI**. Jess: please?!

**JESS**. Lex, watch out!

> (**LEXI** *looks forward.* **HOOKMAN** *pops out of the backseat of the car, his hook raised menacingly. There's a spray of blood.*)

## Scene

(**LEXI** *and* **YOONJI**'s *dorm room.*)

(**LEXI** *paces her room on the phone with her mom, mid-conversation. She adjusts things on her desk and shelves as she talks.*)

**LEXI.** Yeah, I know
   I know she's been calling
   Jess's mom
   I just don't want to bother her, is all!

   –

   Well, if Jess's mom calls and I call her back and nobody answers, then like
   I DO call
   – or I've been meaning to, SOON –
   I just
   Feel like she's got a lot on her plate with the memorial and everything
   AND there's a time difference!

   –

   I'm not blaming you,
   I'm just SAYING!

      (**YOONJI** *enters quickly, gets on her laptop. Awkward.*)

   Can I talk to Dad?

   –

   No, I just want to ask him something.
   Well, just
   Can you tell him when you see him?
   You do see him, right?
   You do live together, don't you?
   No, it's just
   Mom, I'm fine.
   Mom, I am.

LEXI. *(cont.)* Mom, I go out.

   I'm outside right now, as we speak.

   With my friends

   At the Olive Garden.

   Yes, that's a thing.

   They have breadsticks.

      *(YOONJI looks around.)*

   No, I will.

   Yeah, love you, too.

   Say hi to Jess's mom for me tomorrow.

   Tell her I'm sorry I couldn't be there.

   Tell her I had something

   Come up.

      *(LEXI hangs up, finally notices that YOONJI is in the room, too. She shoves her phone into a jacket pocket.)*

   Hey

YOONJI. Hey

   I thought you had class.

LEXI. Hmm? I don't

YOONJI. Don't you normally have class?

LEXI. No

   Or I mean, I do, I just –

   I didn't feel like going.

YOONJI. What happened to your hands?

      *(LEXI looks at her ink-stained hands.)*

LEXI. Nothing.

YOONJI. Nothing?

LEXI. It's probably just my period!

YOONJI. …

LEXI. *(joke)* I get my period and that stuff gets all over!

YOONJI. What?

LEXI. It might've just been a pen.

   I think it was a pen.

**YOONJI**. … okay.

**LEXI**. I'm just having a really bad day

… .

*(a thought)* We broke up.

**YOONJI**. Who?

**LEXI**. Sean. *I* broke up

With him

In a text.

**YOONJI**. Good for you.

**LEXI**. Really?

**YOONJI**. He was kind of old. And weird.

**LEXI**. I think he was a junior?

**YOONJI**. Ew.

**LEXI**. Yeahhhh.

And now my mom's kind of making me feel bad.

**YOONJI**. About what?

**LEXI**. About the memorial.

She wants me to come home, but –

**YOONJI**. You should.

**LEXI**. Should I?

**YOONJI**. You totally

TOTALLY should.

**LEXI**. It's tomorrow.

**YOONJI**. That's perfect.

**LEXI**. For what?

**YOONJI**. Your friend's thing!

**LEXI**. It might not even be that fun.

**YOONJI**. GO.

Who cares if it's fun?

**LEXI**. I guess a memorial

Isn't necessarily gonna be fun.

… but isn't it gonna be really expensive?

**YOONJI**. Fuck that.

**LEXI**. What?

**YOONJI.** Screw them!

**LEXI.** Who?

**YOONJI.** You want to do a shot?

**LEXI.** Of what?

**YOONJI.** I've got Jameson.

**LEXI.** (*"what is Jameson?"*) Okay!

> (**LEXI** and **YOONJI** do a shot of Jameson together.
> A bonding moment. **LEXI** swallows the whiskey,
> makes a face. **YOONJI** pours the rest of the
> Jameson into her peach Snapple. Throughout the
> scene, **YOONJI** discreetly drinks the entire bottle
> of Jameson. **LEXI** doesn't notice. Ideally, we don't
> either.)

**YOONJI.** Go buy it like right now.

**LEXI.** Buy what?

**YOONJI.** Your plane ticket.

**LEXI.** … YEAH!

> (**LEXI** begins the process of buying a plane ticket.)

And can you sign my petition?

**YOONJI.** YEAH!

What's it for?

**LEXI.** It's for drunk driving.

**YOONJI.** Oh, I love drunk driving!

**LEXI.** What?

**YOONJI.** Yeah, I'll totally sign it.

**LEXI.** Cool! Though

I think you can just type it.

> (**YOONJI** types into **LEXI**'s laptop.)

Thanks.

**YOONJI.** No problem.

And you should go out tonight.

**LEXI.** Yeah!

Wait, like OUTSIDE out?

**YOONJI.** Yeah!

**LEXI.** 'Cause I don't

Need to go

OUT outside –

I should probably pack!

> *(But* **YOONJI** *doesn't hear, is already looking through her closet.)*

**YOONJI.** Oooh, you want to wear something really slutty?

**LEXI.** … yeah!

**YOONJI.** Yeah!

> *(***YOONJI** *comes out of the closet with something slutty for* **LEXI** *to wear. She kind of drapes it on top of* **LEXI***, who doesn't put it on but basically just awkwardly sits there with the slutty thing around her shoulders. She waits for* **YOONJI** *to put the slutty thing on her, but* **YOONJI** *is distracted by a book on* **LEXI***'s side of the room and doesn't.)*

Oh, I read this.

**LEXI.** You have?

**YOONJI.** *Year of Magical Thinking?*

Yeah.

When my dad died, my mom bought it for me.

**LEXI.** Was it good?

**YOONJI.** Yeah.

I read the back of it and then I went on Amazon and read the reviews.

But they were really good,

The back of the reviews.

But the point of the book is, like,

If you hope for something enough

Or, like, you do the right thing,

You can make things better.

**LEXI.** Oh, I like that!

**YOONJI**. Yeah, but
　　The point of it is
　　How you can't
　　How you don't
　　How you make a mistake and he follows you forever
　　and there's nothing you can do about it.
　　*(beat)* Though there is that sequel where the daughter
　　dies.

**LEXI**. That can't be what the book is about.

**YOONJI**. *(shrugs)* That's what it said on Amazon.

　　　　*(**YOONJI** gets a text.)*

　　Oh, gotta go!

　　　　*(**LEXI** finally notices that **YOONJI** seems to be
　　　　dressed rather sluttily.)*

**LEXI**. Who're you going out with?

**YOONJI**. Oh, I'm just meeting some friends,
　　Some guys.

**LEXI**. Ooooh, someone's got a date
　　With multiple guys.
　　Do I know them?

**YOONJI**. Maaaaybe.

　　　　*(**LEXI** stares out the window.)*

**LEXI**. You're not going to see that grad student, are you?

**YOONJI**. What?
　　Ew, no.

**LEXI**. Oh good.

　　　　*(**YOONJI** looks at her jacket. It's got red stains on
　　　　it. Blood? Pie?.)*

**YOONJI**. What happened to my jacket?

　　　　*(Wait, is this **LEXI**'s jacket? Oh well. **YOONJI** puts
　　　　it on, downs the last of the Jameson, bundles up for
　　　　the snow.)*

**LEXI.** See you when I get back.

Say hi to multiple guys for me!

**YOONJI.** *(muffled)* Yeahh!

*(YOONJI wobbles out the door in LEXI's jacket. Once YOONJI is gone, LEXI digs into YOONJI's stash of puffy Korean snacks. She reaches for the Jameson bottle, it's empty.)*

**LEXI.** ...

Yoonji?

*(LEXI finds YOONJI's cell phone.)*

Oh, Yoonji, you forgot your –

Cell phone.

*(LEXI has an ominous feeling of foreboding.)*

*(Then LEXI sees YOONJI downstairs walking outside. And someone is following her. Someone like HOOKMAN.)*

Wait, Yoonji... ?

Yoonji?!

*(LEXI races out the door. Oh wait, she has no shoes on. Or jacket. Or scarf. To leave without those would be foolish. LEXI puts on YOONJI's weird Korean jacket and scarf, which don't quite fit. Oh well. Then she grabs the knife, races out the door.)*

## Scene

*(Outside.)*

*(**LEXI** stands in the snow, searching for **YOONJI**. She holds the knife up defensively but then lowers it, feeling silly. **ADAM** walks by, goes to open the door with his keycard. He stops.)*

**ADAM**. You need to be let in?

**LEXI**. No, just –

You're my RA.

Adam?

**ADAM**. Adam.

**LEXI**. Oh thank god!

I need your help.

I heard you could help me!

**ADAM**. You need some right now?

**LEXI**. YES.

**ADAM**. I'm your guy!

How much do you want?

**LEXI**. How much help? I don't know, all of it.

**ADAM**. Okay!

I'll see how much I have left in my room.

**LEXI**. In your room?

**ADAM**. But don't worry. It's the good stuff.

**LEXI**. Are you selling me marijuana?

*(**ADAM** looks left, right.)*

**ADAM**. No?

*(**ADAM** nods: "yes.")*

**LEXI**. I don't want weed, I want you to help me save my friend from the Hookman.

**ADAM**. Ohhhh, okay.

But um, first:

Is he a student?

**LEXI**. He's a serial killer.

**ADAM.** Okay, but is he a student?

'Cause if he's not a student, this might fall outside of the university's jurisdiction.

**LEXI.** Fine, he's a student,

He's a sketchy grad student.

**ADAM.** And is she slutty?

**LEXI.** What kind of question is that?

**ADAM.** Does she give the impression of being someone who might have it coming?

**LEXI.** No!

**ADAM.** Just 'cause the university doesn't really like getting involved in the life and death of its students?

It kind of views it as more of a personal health matter than a disciplinary one.

**LEXI.** No, no, no. My friend is drunk and she needs help.

**ADAM.** Don't worry, I'm sure she'll come around

Sooner or later, she'll see the light.

**LEXI.** I'm not trying to CHANGE her.

I'm trying to SAVE her.

(**ADAM** *gets a text on his phone.*)

**ADAM.** Sorry

I gotta go.

**LEXI.** Wait!

**ADAM.** But hope you find the help you're looking for!

(**LEXI** *blocks his path. At some point during this, she remembers she has the knife.*)

**LEXI.** Listen, I don't know who you are

Or what they pay you

Or what kind of "marijuana" you are selling,

But my roommate went out

So now I am

REQUESTING

(yes.)

That you help me!

(**LEXI** *is unsure whether to raise or lower the knife.*)

**LEXI.** … if that would be okay.

**ADAM.** Oh wait
    Your ROOMMATE

**LEXI.** YES, my roommate!

**ADAM.** Oh, I just saw her!

**LEXI.** Really?!

**ADAM.** She's fine.

**LEXI.** She is?
    And there's not a hook
    For a hand?
    That's gonna – ?

**ADAM.** I don't think so?

**LEXI.** Oh thank god.

**ADAM.** She's waiting for you
    Inside.

**LEXI.** Thank you!

**ADAM.** I'm your guy!

    *(**LEXI** almost goes back inside with **ADAM**.)*

**LEXI.** … I didn't tell you her name.

**ADAM.** You didn't?

**LEXI.** So what's her name,
    If she's okay?

**ADAM.** Well, either she is
    Or she's slutty and she had it coming, so –

**LEXI.** Why would she have it coming?!

**ADAM.** Either way, it's nothing you should worry about.
    Come inside, have a drink,
    Maybe with your top off?

**LEXI.** No.
    I do not think
    I would like that
    Very much.
    …
    NO MEANS NO!

*(**LEXI** fends **ADAM** off with her knife.)*

**ADAM.** What're you afraid of, Lexi?

I'm not that bad, once you get to know me.

**LEXI.** You're my RA,

I thought you were supposed to help me solve my problems.

**ADAM.** No, I'm not.

I'm just the RA.

I'm just the person you call if you get locked out at night.

I don't solve problems,

I just let them in.

*(**LEXI** runs off. When she's far enough off...)*

**LEXI.** And just to let you know, I never went to any of your events!

I just deleted the emails!

*(**LEXI** exits.)*

## Scene

*(Outside.)*

*(A drunken* **YOONJI** *staggers home. She still wears* **LEXI***'s pink jacket and scarf. Her face is obscured by the jacket's hood. A cell phone in the jacket pocket rings.* **YOONJI** *takes out the phone. Weird. Not her phone, but nevertheless… )*

**YOONJI**. *(muffled.)* Hello… ?

*(No response. Then a snowball hits her on the back. She turns.* **HOOKMAN** *stands behind her. Ooh, cute guy. Is he that grad student? He tosses another snowball. She tosses a snowball back. Snowfight!* **HOOKMAN** *runs after* **YOONJI***. He tickles her, she drops the phone.)*

No!

Noooooo!

*(***YOONJI** *laughs. She picks up a handful of snow and smashes it in* **HOOKMAN***'s face.* **HOOKMAN** *wipes off the snow and then chases* **YOONJI***. He grabs her, slits her throat, and rips her face off.* **YOONJI** *screams.)*

*(***HOOKMAN** *stops, breathing heavily. Satisfied, he examines his handiwork. What the hey, this face is Asian! He pulls off* **YOONJI***'s hood/scarf, then looks at* **YOONJI***'s face. Wrong girl. Shoot. He straightens up* **YOONJI***, tries to smoosh the face back on her head. That won't work.* **YOONJI** *flops over into the snow.)*

*(Then he tries to extricate himself from this situation. He shakes the face from his hook. The face momentarily gets stuck on the hook, but eventually falls into a snowbank. He kicks some snow over it. Then* **HOOKMAN** *backs away, runs off, embarrassed.)*

## Scene

*(Outside. Next morning.)*

*(YOONJI – sans face – staggers through the empty quad holding LEXI's jacket, finds a bench, slumps down face first onto the bench. Her faceless face bleeds onto the bench. If it weren't for the blood and lack of face, we would think she's just hung over. The sun rises, LEXI rushes by.)*

**LEXI.** Omigod, Yoonji!

*(YOONJI gurgles a little.)*

Oh hey, did I wake you?

Are you asleep?

Okay, I think you're asleep.

Yeah, you should sleep.

Are you cold?

Here –

*(LEXI covers YOONJI with her own scarf as best she can. A nice moment.)*

Yay.

I found you.

…

I was so afraid I was gonna –

*(CHLOE enters.)*

**CHLOE.** Hey!

**LEXI.** Hey.

**CHLOE.** I am running into you, like, everywhere!

**LEXI.** Yeah.

**CHLOE.** So HOW ARE YOU?

Lexi.

Lexi, right?

**LEXI.** Yeah.

**CHLOE.** See! I was, like,

"Lexi, Lexi: where do you know a Lexi?"

Yoonji's roommate!

How is she?

Is she okay?

**LEXI.** She's right here.

**CHLOE.** 'Cause I hear the hookmen this year have been CRAZY!

**LEXI.** Wait, what?

**CHLOE.** I'm just hanging up fliers for our thing.

**LEXI.** Oh, okay.

> *(**CHLOE** hands **LEXI** a flier.)*

**CHLOE.** It's gonna benefit someone,
Probably me.

> *(**CHLOE** grasps **LEXI**'s hands in solidarity.)*

But lemme know about your fashion show.

**LEXI.** Fashion show?

**CHLOE.** Don't you have a fashion show?
That you're in
… or that you're doing something with?

> *(**CHLOE** gives **LEXI** a "maybe there's something you do in life that I'm thinking of?" look.)*

**LEXI.** I don't really know what I want to be in
Or doing something with
At this point in time.

**CHLOE.** Oh
Okay.
…
But coffee?

**LEXI.** Sure.
When? Now?

**CHLOE.** COFFEE, *yes.*

**LEXI.** You didn't answer my question

**CHLOE.** I didn't?

LEXI. *(deliberately)* Do you want to get coffee right now?

(**CHLOE** *makes a small unintelligible noise.*)

CHLOE. I am just so busy!

(**LEXI** *has a small revelation.*)

LEXI. We're not getting coffee.

CHLOE. *("no")* We're not getting coffee.

LEXI. Why not?

CHLOE. Because you're not the type of person I get coffee with.

Because I don't find you that interesting.

LEXI. Oh.

CHLOE. Is that more of what you were looking for?

LEXI. I guess.

CHLOE. See? That's what happens when you start asking questions:

You learn the things that you don't really want to hear.

LEXI. *(suddenly)* You've got a small head.*

CHLOE. Huh?

LEXI. Your head's just really [small].

CHLOE. You're probably right.

Oh! And here.

(**CHLOE** *takes out an ID card, tosses it to* **LEXI**.)

LEXI. What?

CHLOE. We found it last night.

I figured Yoonji might want it back.

LEXI. This isn't Yoonji.

CHLOE. I know.

LEXI. Wait, this is a fake.

What would she want with a fake?

CHLOE. I don't know. Maybe you should ask her.

---

*This can be changed to "large," depending on the actor's head in relation to the head of the actor playing **LEXI**.

*(CHLOE peeks at YOONJI's face. LEXI looks, too.*
*What the hey! Where'd her face go?!)*

**LEXI.** Oh my god, her face!

What happened to her face?!

**CHLOE.** Don't worry, I'm sure she'll sober up.

She came by our thing last night, she was totally wasted.

Looks like she forgot to take her contacts out.

**LEXI.** She lost her face!

**CHLOE.** Koreans! Right?

I hear that happens a lot freshman year.

You lose face and it all goes downhill from there!

**LEXI.** No, seriously, her face is GONE.

**CHLOE.** Yeah, I think something might've happened after she left.

**LEXI.** Then why didn't you help?

**CHLOE.** I know, right?!

I am just SO BUSY.

**LEXI.** You're a terrible person.

**CHLOE.** Oh come on,

We all knew that would happen.

**LEXI.** We did?

**CHLOE.** She was a total alcoholic

… or did you not see him coming?

**LEXI.** You mean "it."

**CHLOE.** No, I mean "him."

**LEXI.** What?

**CHLOE.** Anyway!

Her mom's here to pick her up.

They've been looking for her everywhere.

*(to* **YOONJI***)* Yoonji.

> *(CHLOE shakes* **YOONJI***.* **YOONJI** *gurgles a little.)*

*(to* **YOONJI***)* They're in the dean's office.

> *(***YOONJI** *gets up, grabs the fake ID, wanders off.)*

**LEXI**. What is this?! What is going on?!

**CHLOE**. My brother says it happens all the time freshman
     year.

**LEXI**. But I was gonna save her.

     I was supposed to save her…

**CHLOE**. Listen, Lex:

     When I killed my little sister,

     The exact same thing happened to me,

     But I learned not to think about it.

**LEXI**. "When you killed your little sister?!"

     What does that even mean?

**CHLOE**. Like I said:

     I don't really think about it.

     The truth is what you make of it!

     Sometimes these things happen

     And there's nothing you can do to make it better.

**LEXI**. That's not true.

     I'm going to go home

     I'm going to say my speech

     I'm going to help my friend

     And I'm going to make things better!

     'Cause It Gets Better!

**CHLOE**. Good luck with that.

     Oh! And your friend says hi.

        (**CHLOE** *mimes something like "hook for a hand."*)

The one with a [noise] for a something?

He said he's coming by

To get you later.

But anyway – !

It was nice knowing you.

And have fun with your life!

You're gonna need it.

        (**CHLOE** *exits.*)

## Scene

*(Outside the auditorium at West Porter High.)*

**(KAYLEIGH** *stands in front of the closed auditorium doors with programs. She wears a nametag and an honor society hat, which is an important but ultimately stupid-looking hat. She texts.* **LEXI** *hurries down the hall with her knife. She waits for* **KAYLEIGH** *to open the door.)*

**LEXI.** Heyyy

*(***KAYLEIGH** *looks up, hands her a program.)*

**KAYLEIGH.** Mm.

**LEXI.** I need to get in.

**KAYLEIGH.** They're doing the memorial.

**LEXI.** Right. That's why I'm here.

I have a speech.

*(***LEXI** *holds up her crappy looking speech.)*

See?

…

I need to get in.

**KAYLEIGH.** You're late.

**LEXI.** There was fog on the runway.

**KAYLEIGH.** Yeah, but now you can't go in.

No late entry for students.

**LEXI.** I'm not a student.

**KAYLEIGH.** You look like a student.

**LEXI.** Well, I'm not.

**KAYLEIGH.** Where do I know you from?

Did you used to go here?

**LEXI.** *(slightly annoyed)* Yes. I did.

I'm Lexi. Lexi Gellner.

**KAYLEIGH.** Oh! Lexi.

**LEXI.** YES. Lexi.

So now can I get in?

**KAYLEIGH.** *(listens)* Hold on.

Almost.

Maybe when they get to a break.

**LEXI.** Fine.

> (**LEXI** *waits by the door.* **KAYLEIGH** *texts.* **LEXI**
> *tries to see what* **KAYLEIGH** *is texting.* **KAYLEIGH**
> *notices this and* **LEXI** *pretends she isn't looking.*)

I have that hat.

I have that same hat.

**KAYLEIGH.** Yeah?

**LEXI.** From when I went here.

Are you a freshman?

**KAYLEIGH.** *(preens)* I'm a sophomore.

**LEXI.** Oh, cool.

…

Are you taking AP Euro this year?

**KAYLEIGH.** I have Mr. Granucci.

**LEXI.** Oh! I had him.

**KAYLEIGH.** He talks about you sometimes.

He said you were a really good student.

> (**LEXI** *preens, makes a "who, me?" face/noise.*)

You went to UConn, right?

**LEXI.** Yeah.

**KAYLEIGH.** So can I ask you?

Is it hard to get in to UConn?

**LEXI.** Um

**KAYLEIGH.** I heard it wasn't hard to get in,

That all you need're okay SAT scores.

How come you didn't go to a UC?

**LEXI.** I applied to UConn and I got in?

**KAYLEIGH.** Is it weird being in college and still not having
any friends?

Does that happen to a lot of people?

**LEXI.** Who said I don't
  What?

**KAYLEIGH.** It's just a question,
  You don't have to answer if you don't like what the
  answer is.
  I'm just asking.
  (No offense... )
  You want a program?

**LEXI.** I *have* a program.

> (**KAYLEIGH** *thinks she hears something inside the
> auditorium.*)

**KAYLEIGH.** And if you're gonna stand there,
  You need to stand in line

**LEXI.** I am in line.

**KAYLEIGH.** Like over there.
  'Cause you can't be facing the door when they open it.

> (**LEXI** *tries to look more line-like.*)

  Yeah, they're almost at a break.
  The best friend is almost done.

**LEXI.** What best friend?

**KAYLEIGH.** Her best friend.

**LEXI.** No, no, no, no, I'M the best friend.

**KAYLEIGH.** That's not what I heard.

**LEXI.** Look:
  I don't even want to be here!

**KAYLEIGH.** Then what're you doing here?

**LEXI.** I'm HERE for Jess.
  I'm doing this for Jess.

**KAYLEIGH.** I thought she was dead.

**LEXI.** She is!

**KAYLEIGH.** Then how can you do something for her if she's
  already dead?

**LEXI**. I don't know, but can you just let me in?
  I'm trying to make things better!
  And you're kind of making it worse!

**KAYLEIGH**. I'm just standing here.

**LEXI**. I know.

**KAYLEIGH**. I'm just a sophomore.

**LEXI**. Right, YES
  But –

**KAYLEIGH**. You're the one making a scene.

**LEXI**. How? Am I making a scene?!

> (**KAYLEIGH** *shrugs. Then* **KAYLEIGH** *notices the blood on* **LEXI** *'s shirt.*)

**KAYLEIGH**. Are you bleeding?

**LEXI**. No.

**KAYLEIGH**. Okay, but
  If you are, you kind of can't come in.

> (**KAYLEIGH** *gestures to* **LEXI**. *Blood from* **JESS** *'s death or* **YOONJI** *'s death or someone somewhere has gotten all over* **LEXI** *throughout the course of the play.*)

**LEXI**. This isn't even my own blood.

**KAYLEIGH**. Okay, but
  Even if it's not even your own blood,
  You still might also not be allowed to come in,
  Just 'cause you're also not allowed to kill people either.

**LEXI**. I didn't kill anyone.

**KAYLEIGH**. Are you sure?
  'Cause that's not what I heard.
  I heard you were nothing
  But a stupid
  Irresponsible
  Spineless little bitch.
  At least that's what my mom said.

**LEXI**. I don't like you.

I don't like how people who go to this school are anymore.

We weren't like this when we went here.

Our class was the best class.

**KAYLEIGH**. They say that every year.

**LEXI**. Why would they do that?!

**KAYLEIGH**. I don't know,

I'm just a sophomore.

> (**LEXI** *drops a book she's been carrying.* **KAYLEIGH** *notices the book.*)

Oh, I read that.

**LEXI**. *(skeptical)* Oh really.

**KAYLEIGH**. *Year of Magical Thinking?* Yeah.

**LEXI**. Like you saw it on a plane or you read the front back of it on Amazon.

**KAYLEIGH**. No, *I read it.*

Did you like it?

**LEXI**. *("shoot, I should've read it on the plane")* Yeah, it was… really uplifting.

**KAYLEIGH**. For me, reading it,

It was just comforting to know that no matter how much you lose,

You can always lose more.

Like

No matter how bad things get,

They can always get worse.

**LEXI**. No.

**KAYLEIGH**. What?

**LEXI**. No. That's not true.

**KAYLEIGH**. … or maybe you haven't gotten to that part yet.

**LEXI**. Open This Door.

**KAYLEIGH**. Why?

**LEXI**. Because
   She was my friend,
   She was my best friend,
   And I think of her all the time.
   I'll be in the shower
   Or the hall.
   I'll be looking at a dog,
   And I'll be like,
   "Oh a dog,"
   "Oh I should tell Jess,"
   "Oh I should tell Jess when I see her tomorrow."
   But I can't,
   'Cause I won't.
   And I know what I'm thinking isn't necessarily the most interesting
   Or useful-to-society thing,
   But I have these thoughts,
   These stupid little thoughts,
   And I don't know what I'm supposed to do with them if you don't fucking open this door for me right now.

**KAYLEIGH**. Are you threatening me?

**LEXI**. YES.

**KAYLEIGH**. Well, good for you, Lexi.
   Good for you.

**LEXI**. … thank you.

   (**KAYLEIGH** *backs away from the door.*)

**KAYLEIGH**. Have fun.
   Just remember: you might not like what you find in there.

**LEXI**. What?

   (**KAYLEIGH** *takes the program from* **LEXI**.)

**KAYLEIGH**. Your guilt is what you make of it.

(**LEXI** *pushes past* **KAYLEIGH**, *pulls open the doors. On the other side is* **JESS** *in the passenger seat of the car.*)

**LEXI**. What is this?

**KAYLEIGH**. This is what happens when you don't see it the first time.

It always comes back around in the end.

(**KAYLEIGH** *points forward.* **LEXI** *walks into the next scene, takes her place.*)

### Scene

*(In the car.)*

**(JESS** *in the passenger seat,* **LEXI** *in the driver's seat, with In 'N Out as before. The metal scraping noise.)*

**JESS.** What was that?

**LEXI.** What

**JESS.** That noise.

You didn't hear that?

**LEXI.** I didn't hear anything that sounded like that noise.

**JESS.** It was like

A scraping?

**LEXI.** No?

**JESS.** I was gonna say something.

I don't remember, but it was two things…

**LEXI.** It was otters.

**JESS.** YES. Otters.

So I was watching this video the other day that my brother showed me.

And otters:

They hold hands when they sleep.

**LEXI.** With each other?!

**JESS.** Yeah!

To keep from drifting away.

**LEXI.** *("psh!")* No!

**JESS.** YES.

"Otters holding hands."

Look it up.

They hold hands while they sleep so they won't float away from,

I don't know,

The otter clump.

**LEXI.** But what if they both float away?

JESS. Yeah, but at least then
    They'd still be [together],
    You know?
    I mean, how many otters do you need to be an otter?

LEXI. One, I guess.

    …

    I like that.
    Why don't we do that?
    Why don't people holds hands?

JESS. I think we do.

LEXI. I wish someone would hold my hand,
    To keep me from drifting away from myself.

        (**LEXI** *holds her own hand to demonstrate.*)

    You know?

        (**JESS** *takes* **LEXI***'s hand. They hold hands limply as otters might.*)

JESS. Yeah.

LEXI. Look! We're otters.
    We have otter hands.

JESS. Otter hands!

        (*They make a noise that indicates "hands!" They hold hands throughout the rest of the scene.*)

    We'll watch the video when you drop me off with the Davis people,
    We'll watch it real fast.

LEXI. Okay.

JESS. *(beat)* Do we, though?

LEXI. What?

JESS. Watch the video?

LEXI. No. We don't.

JESS. Lex, watch out!

        (**LEXI** *and the rest of the car is suddenly bathed in a red light.*)

**LEXI.** *(realizes)* The red light.

  *I* went through the red light.

  It wasn't the drunk guy,

  It was me.

> *(JESS is mortally wounded. Maybe shrapnel sticks out of her. She oozes blood as she tries to breathe.)*

Jess?

> *(LEXI tries to snap JESS out of it.)*

Jess, no.

Jess, please.

Jess, c'mon.

> *(JESS gurgles. It's a brutal, bloody death.)*

I'm gonna go get help.

I'm gonna be right back!

> *(LEXI tries to escape the car, but JESS holds onto her hand.)*

**JESS.** No.

**LEXI.** No?

> *(JESS clutches LEXI's hand more tightly.)*

**JESS.** Don't you want to see what happened?

  Don't you want to see what you did?

  "People who kill people should be punished.

  People who kill people should not be allowed to LIVE with their lives."

**LEXI.** I didn't MEAN that

  I didn't mean that to mean me!

> *(More blood spurts out of JESS. LEXI claws at the door of the car with her free hand.)*

Jess, stop.

Jess, let go.

**JESS.** But we're otters.

  We have otter hands.

**LEXI**. Jess, that hurts.

**JESS**. Of course it hurts.

**LEXI**. Why're you doing this?

**JESS**. I'm just trying to help you see.

> (*The light begin to flicker.*)

**LEXI**. Wait, Jess
    Jess?
    I'm sorry.
    I'm so sorry.

> (*The lights flicker a final time.* **JESS** *has disappeared and now* **HOOKMAN** *sits in* **JESS**'s *chair.* **LEXI** *looks over at* **HOOKMAN**.)

You're not Jess.

> (**HOOKMAN** *shakes his head.*)

You're that guy
With the hook
For a hand.

> (**HOOKMAN** *lunges, hook-first, at* **LEXI**. *She fights him with her knife, and screams.* **HOOKMAN** *smashes his hook into the dashboard of the car. It gets stuck. He pulls too hard. His hook comes off, so he just has a stump for a hand.*)

Omigod, your hand!

> (**LEXI** *dislodges the hook from the dashboard. She almost gives it back to* **HOOKMAN**, *but thinks better of this and keeps it. She brandishes the knife and the hook.*)

What is this?
What do you want from me?!

> (**HOOKMAN** *takes out a phone, holds it up. It begins to ring.* **LEXI** *listens.*)

Oh
My phone.

**LEXI.** *(cont.)* You want me to

Oh.

That.

Um

Can you get that for me?

My hands're kind of gross.

**HOOKMAN.** *("right")*

> (**HOOKMAN** *answers the phone for* **LEXI,** *holds it up to her ear.* **LEXI** *wipes off her hand, hands* **HOOKMAN** *the weapons so she can continue to drive and talk on the phone. He screws his hook back on. As she speaks, we begin to see that it is daytime.)*

**LEXI.** Hi, Mom.

No, I'm in the car.

No, I'm driving.

No, I'm with someone else.

   –

Sorry, I meant to tell you.

No, I'm going to Jess's.

I'm going to Jess's mom.

I just

Need to tell her something.

   –

Yeah.

Okay, I gotta go.

We'll be home soon.

We'll see you later.

> (**LEXI** *drives.* **HOOKMAN** *sits next to her in the passenger seat.)*

## Scene

*(Epilogue.)*

**(CHLOE** *comes out with her giant thermos of coffee. She sees us. Confidentially… )*

CHLOE. I die, too.

Of food poisoning!

FOOD POISONING.

I know, right?!

**(CHLOE** *laughs, looks around. Maybe we the audience aren't there? Hm. Is she talking to a wall?)*

WHO am I talking to?

Am I talking to anyone?

Anyone?!

I turn around and it's like

WHY am I talking to this *wall?!*

Aaaanyway

I think that's the end.

I think the end is that we all die.

That's always the end, right?

DEAD!

DIE!

YOU!

**(CHLOE** *mimes getting slashed by Hookman laughs, then exhales.)*

Aaaahhhhhh.

**(CHLOE** *takes a swig of coffee. But it's sadly empty. She shows us how it is empty: "See! Life!")*

Yep.

**(CHLOE** *shrugs, exits.)*

**End**